HENRY'S MAP

David Elliot

Philomel Books • An Imprint of Penguin Group (USA) Inc.

PHILOMEL BOOKS

A division of Penguin Young Readers Group.   Published by The Penguin Group.

Penguin Group (USA) Inc., 375 Hudson Street, New York, NY 10014, U.S.A.

Penguin Group (Canada), 90 Eglinton Avenue East, Suite 700, Toronto, Ontario M4P 2Y3, Canada
(a division of Pearson Penguin Canada Inc.).

Penguin Books Ltd, 80 Strand, London WC2R 0RL, England.

Penguin Ireland, 25 St. Stephen's Green, Dublin 2, Ireland (a division of Penguin Books Ltd).

Penguin Group (Australia), 707 Collins Street, Melbourne, Victoria 3008, Australia
(a division of Pearson Australia Group Pty Ltd).

Penguin Books India Pvt Ltd, 11 Community Centre, Panchsheel Park, New Delhi–110 017, India.

Penguin Group (NZ), 67 Apollo Drive, Rosedale, Auckland 0632, New Zealand
(a division of Pearson New Zealand Ltd).

Penguin Books South Africa, Rosebank Office Park, 181 Jan Smuts Avenue, Parktown North 2193, South Africa.

Penguin China, B7 Jiaming Center, 27 East Third Ring Road North, Chaoyang District, Beijing 100020, China.

Penguin Books Ltd, Registered Offices: 80 Strand, London WC2R 0RL, England.

Edited by Tamra Tuller.   Design by Semadar Megged.   Text set in 16-pt. Neutraface Text.
The illustrations are rendered in pencil and watercolor.
Library of Congress Cataloging-in-Publication Data is available upon request.

ISBN 978-0-399-16072-1
1 3 5 7 9 10 8 6 4 2

ALWAYS LEARNING   PEARSON

For my sister Karen,
who loves maps.

Henry was a very organized sort of pig.
He liked knowing exactly where
everything was in his tidy little sty.

He straightened his mirror and smiled.
"A place for everything and everything in its
place," he said.

Henry looked out his window and frowned.
Tsk, tsk. What a mess the farm was!
How could anybody ever find anything out there?
Then he had an idea.

"I shall make a map," he said, "so that everyone will know what belongs where."

He went to his cupboard for his pencil and some paper and trotted to his table.

The first thing he drew was his sty. And he drew a picture of himself next to it.

HENRYS
STY

HENRY

Then he rolled up his map and marched outside.

At the woolshed, he came across Maisie, Daisy, and Clementine.

"Baaa. What are you doing, Henry?" they asked.

"I'm making a map of the farm," said Henry.

"Ooh, how exciting," cried the sheep. "Are we in it?"

"You are right here," said Henry. And he drew a square for the woolshed with three sheep beside it.

The sheep clapped their hooves together.

Henry walked across the meadow and came upon Abigail sitting in the shade of a large oak tree.

"Hello, Henry. What are you doing?" asked Abigail.

But before he could answer, the sheep cried, "Baaa! He's making a map of the farm. And we're in it!"

"Really?" said Abigail. "Can I be in it, too?"

"Certainly," said Henry. And he drew a scribbly circle for the oak tree and a picture of a cow.

Abbigail

Tree

Henry continued on his way until he saw
Mr. Brown grazing by his stable.

"Hello, Henry. What are you doing?" neighed
Mr. Brown.

Maisie, Daisy, Clementine, and Abigail quickly
shouted, "He's making a map! And we're all in it!"

"Remarkable," snorted Mr. Brown. "Is there room
for a horse?"

"Of course," said Henry. He took out his pencil and
drew a square for the stable and a picture of a horse.

By the time Henry arrived at the chicken coop, all the animals were in an uproar.

"A map! Henry's making a map! And we're all in it!" they exclaimed.

He drew a square for the coop and three chickens.

"Now," he said proudly, "we'll know where everything is."

"Follow me!" said Henry, leading the other
animals up the hill. "I'll show you my map."

HENRYS
STY

Woolshed

HENRY

sheep

HENRYS
MAP

Abbigail

Tree

Mr Brown

Stabel

Chicken
Coop

All the animals looked at the farm. Then they looked
at the map. And then they looked at the farm again.

"But we're not there," bleated the sheep.

"We're gone," whinnied Mr. Brown.

"Oh no!" mooed Abigail.

"Where did we go?" squawked the chickens.

Henry looked out at the empty farm. There was
no sign of the animals from his map.

Down the hill they dashed, Henry leading
the way, clutching his map.

He rushed to the chicken coop, staring at his map.
"There should be hens right here," he said.
"Here we are," puffed the hens, running up behind him.
"Thank goodness!" said Henry.

He ran on to the stable.
"Mr. Brown!" he called.
"I'm right here," snorted Mr. Brown.
"What a relief!" gasped Henry.

"Abigail?" he yelled when he reached the oak tree.
"Coming," mooed Abigail, running to her tree.
"Thank heavens," said Henry.

"But what about those sheep?"

"Here we are!" cried the sheep, dancing on the woolshed steps. "Your map was right after all, Henry."

But Henry needed to be sure.

He hurried back to his sty and
threw open the door.
   There was no one inside!

He tiptoed over to his mirror. Slowly, he looked into it.

"There you are, Henry." He smiled.

"Just where you ought to be."

A place for everything and everything in its place.